THE
bee
AND THE
rose

peter
de rosa

ARGUS COMMUNICATIONS   Niles, Illinois 60648

ARGUS COMMUNICATIONS
7440 Natchez Avenue
Niles, Illinois 60648

International Standard Book Number:
0-913592-54-4
Library of Congress Catalog Card Number:
75-7543

1 2 3 4 5 6 7 8 9 0

This book is for the rose
who gave me a name
and unfolded me
in my hour of need.

A story about little people
in every place
and every walk of life
who are pushed around
by big institutions

In the beginning Bobby Bee had not been unhappy. That was because he didn't know then what happiness was. But as soon as he began to suspect that life held out other, richer possibilities . . . . Well, let me tell you the whole story.

Bobby was only a beginner in the Spring. At first, he liked the hive he lived in. In fact, he felt very proud of it.

He was told—he forgot who told him—that he was born to be a forager. His job was to go out and visit the flowers and gather both the nectar that turns into delicious honey and the pollen that feeds the unhatched eggs.

He remembered the initial thrill of stepping outside the hive. It was a bright, sunny morning in April, and there were beads of dew upon the grass.

One of the doorkeepers at the threshold of the hive said to him before he spread his gossamer wings for his trial flight:

"Number 15/753. Your life is very short. Remember one thing: **Be useful**."

Bobby wasn't called Bobby at that time. I'll explain later on how he got this name. When he was hatched he was given only a number. Since he was the 15,753rd to be hatched, "15/753" was how he was known.

On this first eventful morning, the explorer bees had returned soon after dawn with news of a luscious bed of primroses nearby and some rich, fragrant yellow bushes that needed prompt attention.

I must remember instructions, thought Bobby, making sure his antennae were in good working order. Life is very short. I must be **useful.** He kept repeating: I must be **useful.**

He was dispatched to the primroses. In an hour he had visited about a hundred flowers. He was feeling very pleased with himself at the haul of nectar he had gathered in his first stomach. This stomach belonged to the hive because everything contained in it had to be emptied out on his return.

"15/753 reporting back, sir," he said to the doorkeeper who kept the books.

"How many flowers did you visit?" asked the doorkeeper gruffly.

"About a hundred, sir," said Bobby proudly.

"About?" cried the doorkeeper. And then louder, "**About**?" He sounded angry, but he wasn't really. In his rule book it said he **had** to raise his voice like that. "I want the **exact** number. Exactness is everything. You are failing in your duty, 15/753."

"I think it was . . . ."

"Don't **think,** 15/753. Don't think in **any sense.** That is the way to disaster. First principle: **Do! Don't think!**

"Next time . . . ." began Bobby.

"Next time is now," roared the doorkeeper with a perfectly pitched, regulation roar. "Empty that sack immediately and bring in 210 flowers-full in the next hour."

That was the beginning of Bobby's apprenticeship.

Remember it was April, a month before the flowers are in blossom, before the cabbages have grown. To return with 210 flowers-full in a single hour in that frugal season when flowers are rare was hard work, I can tell you. But Bobby managed it. Just. Even so, the doorkeeper did not

compliment him. He just told him to empty out his sack into a big vessel and get to work again. There were no coffee-breaks.

Only at night was there rest. After the day's fierce sunlight and the fresh air it was a bit crowded and dark inside the hive. But how proud Bobby was of this splendid and well-ordered home.

Every bee had his own special job to do. Some beat their wings to heat the air in the cool nights and, he imagined, to dry up the water that clung to the honey. There were the cleaners who swept up all the rubbish and the droppings. Then there were the plumbers and the repair men. Deep inside the inner sanctum, hidden from any prying eyes, was the Queen.

Everyone had the fixed aim: to be useful. And the whole hive worked smoothly and peacefully day and night.

One morning, Bobby had been visiting a nice patch of clover with 19/201. The two bees were not friends —for friendship in the hive was forbidden—but they had worked together for three whole weeks without even a Sunday off.

Somewhere on the journey 19/201 had injured a leg, and one of his wings was slightly crumpled. In the last stage of the journey home Bobby did his best to lighten the load of his fellow-bee.

He wasn't even sure himself of his motive for helping him but he suspected it was not altogether honorable. I may be helping 19/201, he thought, because I am feeling sorry for him—and, as he well knew, sympathy was strictly forbidden. It led to inefficiency; and inefficiency threatened the future.

"19/201," yelled the officious doorkeeper, "Keep out!" The antennae of the doorkeeper were not waving slightly with acknowledgement as they

usually did when one of the members of the hive returned. They stood straight up fiercely, challengingly, as if poor 19/201 were a thief or a tramp or an enemy.

19/201 pleaded to be permitted to enter.

"Not allowed." said the doorkeeper. "It's against the regulations."

"Whose regulations?" queried 19/201 in obvious pain from his injuries. But for his sufferings, he would never have asked such a silly, rebellious question.

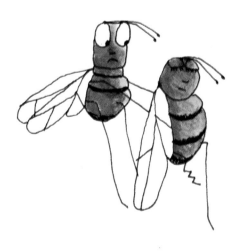

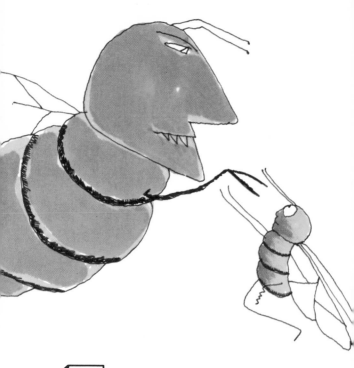

The doorkeeper did not seem to hear the question. He was content to repeat: "It's against the regulations." His way of being useful was by insisting on the regulations, and Bobby thought he should be admired for doing his job so faithfully.

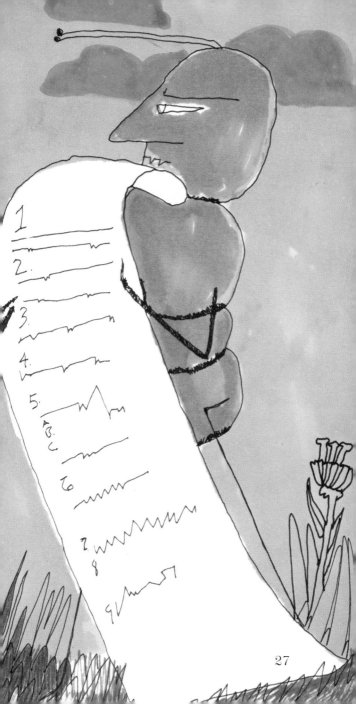

27

When 19/201 tried to squeeze in through the front door the doorkeeper called upon the guards who ejected him by force.

"The regulations say," the doorkeeper spoke the words without any hard feelings, or feelings of any sort, "no injured bee may be allowed to re-enter the hive." Then he turned to Bobby: "I saw you, 15/753, assisting the injured 19/201."

"I'm sorry, sir," said Bobby, "but I assure you I was only concerned about the pollen that 19/201 was carrying. I thought it was a shame to waste it." He wasn't certain if this was true or not.

"Nothing can be worse than breaking regulations," said the doorkeeper. "Nothing."

"It won't happen again, sir," said Bobby trembling.

The doorkeeper noticed Bobby was trembling. "You are afraid 15/753."

"Really, sir, I'm not, sir. It was just that I perspired freely on the journey and I felt a little chilled waiting for permission to enter."

"Eliminate all emotions," said the doorkeeper. "They are all dangerous. If you keep your heart pure, you will never be afraid. Be pure, be faithful, be USEFUL."

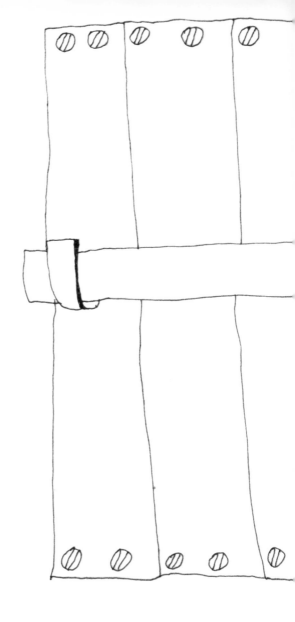

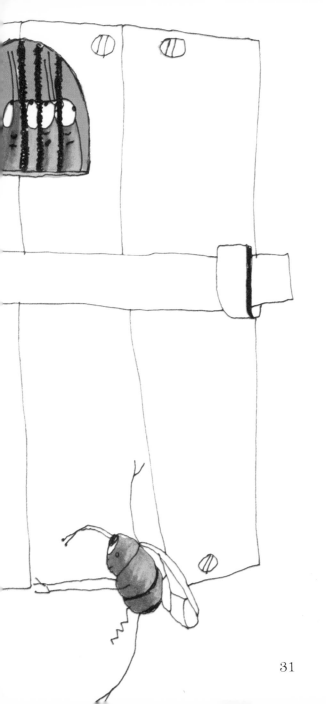

Bobby promised all these things and emptied his sack. Then, careful to take no heed of the screams of 19/201 who was suffering from pain and exile, he returned—in a beeline, naturally—to the field of clover.

I mustn't think about 19/201, he told himself. The regulations must be correct. Haven't we gone on for centuries by following regulations? If we went against the regulations only once . . . . . The possibilities were too terrible to contemplate. Besides, Bobby

was doing what was forbidden: thinking. I must be useful, he said to himself.

He never saw 19/201 again. He was afraid he might miss him just a little. But he was very confused. It was wrong to miss him. It was wrong to be afraid he **might** miss him, or, for that matter, to be afraid he might not miss him. With all these regulations telling you what was the only right thing, it was so easy to do wrong.

April passed. It was a good month as Aprils go. Thousands of drums and vats of honey were already filled. Bobby stifled the question which arose in him: What's it all for? He knew he could live comfortably on what he found in one or two flowers, and it was a puzzle to him why his quota had now been raised to 250 each hour.

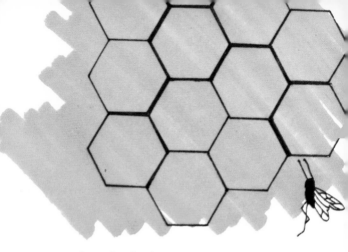

Inside the hive the honeyed walls were separated from each other by golden corridors and linked by passageways, all designed by the most brilliant architects and carried out by the cleverest engineers. It was so geometrically correct Bobby felt ashamed he had ever asked himself what it was all for, or wondered, if only slightly, whether the regulations might do with the occasional alteration.

May and June were such cold months that many worker-bees died. Bobby noticed that no one tried to bury them. They just lay there in piles, stiff and dry, with ants running all over them.

Bobby knew it would be wrong to pity the dead, and futile to cover them with leaves or erect memorials for them on his own. The rules of the hive did not allow pity or burial rites. And the rules . . . well, they **had** to be right, didn't they? There was no point in being a bee if they were wrong, and how can a bee be anything but a bee?

One glorious afternoon in July, Bobby dived headlong into a bright red rose.

"Did I give you permission to enter?" inquired a tinkling voice.

Bobby wasn't used to being addressed by flowers.

"I asked you a question, young fellow," said the tinkling voice once more, and now Bobby was sure it was the bright red rose who was speaking to him.

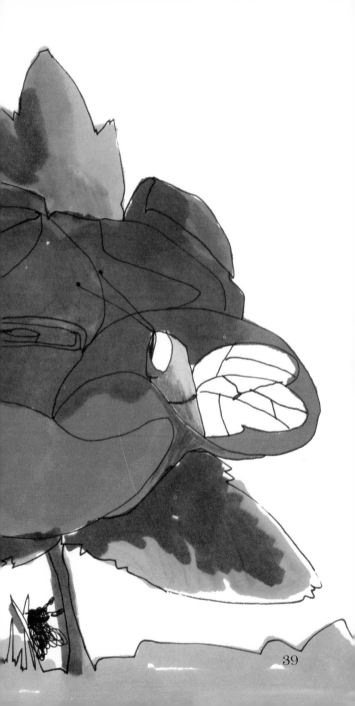

"I'm very sorry, miss," said Bobby. "Roses haven't raised any objection before."

"Well, there's always a first time."

"Oh dear," said Bobby, "I wonder what the doorkeeper will say."

Since Bobby seemed so distressed, the rose, thinking it might be her fault, tried to cheer him up. "May I know your name?" she asked.

"I'm 15/753."

"That's not a name," said the rose. "That's a number."

"It's the only name I've got," replied Bobby sadly.

"Then I will call you Bobby."

Bobby said, "You mustn't do that, miss."

"My name is Rosa."

"You mustn't do that, Rosa," Bobby repeated, charmed despite himself by the flower's lovely name.

"And why mustn't I?"

"Because it's against the regulations."

"Who," said Rosa, "made such silly regulations, Bobby?"

"Call me 15/753."

"Certainly not."

41

Bobby could see he wouldn't make her change her mind.

"I must be off," said Bobby. "The doorkeeper . . . ."

"The doorkeeper must be a tyrant," Rosa interrupted with a scornful laugh. But before the laugh had stopped ringing Bobby was on his way home to the hive.

What an extraordinary creature this Rosa is, he told himself. First, she wants me to ask permission to do what the regulations **order** me to do. Then she gives me a name as if I were someone special. Next, she even makes a joke of the regulations and calls our loyal doorkeeper a tyrant.

Secretly, so secretly that Bobby himself didn't notice it, he rather liked the new name Rosa had given him. Yet he was worried by some of the things Rosa had said because . . . well, because for some time he had half wanted to say them himself.

he next morning, Bobby flew directly to the rosebush on which Rosa grew. Before he had time to open his mouth Rosa said:

"You can come in if you like. There's quite a lot I want to ask you."

Bobby entered shyly.

"Do you ever have a day off?" asked Rosa.

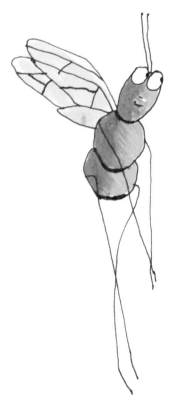

"Not exactly," answered Bobby.

"Not even Sundays and holidays?"

"No."

"I thought not," said Rosa in her musical voice. "You have the look of a slave."

"I think I'll be flying on," said Bobby.

"You can't bear the truth about yourself," Rosa said but not unkindly.

"Tell me, why do you always travel in a beeline?"

"Because it's the shortest way to go."

"Why can't you go by the longest way?"

"But that's silly to go by the longest way when there's a shortcut."

"That's just where you're wrong, Bobby," Rosa insisted. "Haven't you ever watched the butterflies? Why can't you be carefree as they are? Surely you can see the fun they get by traveling backwards and forwards, up and down."

"What is **fun**?" asked Bobby.

"**Fun** is doing something because you like doing it and for no other reason."

"Then," said Bobby, "how would we gather all the honey in if we stopped for **fun**?"

"Let me ask you a question first, Bobby," Rosa said. "Why are you gathering in all that honey?"

"Because the rules say we must."

"But isn't there a reason for the rules?"

Bobby said, "There must be a reason but perhaps only the One who made the rules understands it."

"Not very convincing," Rosa went
on. "I've been told that when your
beehive is full of honey everyone leaves
in one great swarm and sets off in
search of another hive—all colorless
and empty. Where's the sense in that?"

"You are trying to undermine my
faith," said Bobby angrily—except he
remembered the doorkeeper's words
that if he were pure of heart he would
never feel anger or emotion of any sort.
Perhaps he was half enjoying Rosa's
temptations.

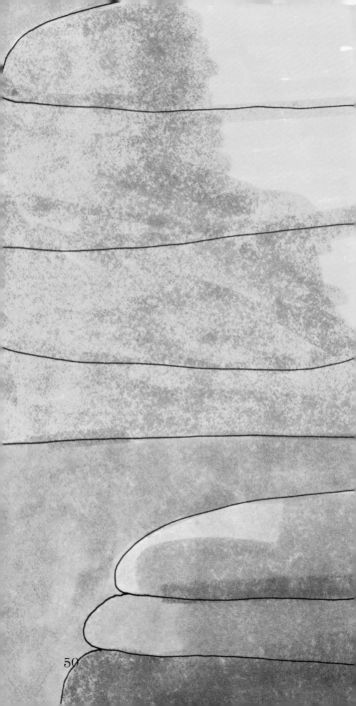

Rosa was saying, "And who is this Someone who makes the rules you have to obey?"

"I don't know," Bobby said, "but he must have been very wise because everything in the hive always works so perfectly."

"Always the same you mean."

"Isn't that the same as perfectly?"

"No, it isn't," said Rosa. "If

everything is always the same then there's no chance of improvement, is there?"

"But that's because everything is **already** perfect."

"Bobby, you can't believe that."

Bobby—to quench the sparks of unbelief that were shooting up inside him—shouted, "Of course, I believe it!" and buzzed off to another flower.

In his heart, Bobby wasn't sure any more what he believed. Was it **perfection** not to allow the bruised and broken bees to return to the hive? Was it perfection for his race never to bury their dead? Was it perfection to have no leisure, no holidays, no **fun**? Was it perfection to live always in darkness with thousands in a single room?

Questions. He was full of questions.

After his regulation time Bobby returned to the barracks and announced he had visited 120 flowers. The doorkeeper reported him for inefficiency to the head forager bee.

The head forager was very long and dark and lean. He was the hardest worker among all the bees and he looked furious. But when he gave poor Bobby 3 bad marks for inefficiency, he was all regulation smiles.

"First offence, 15/753," he said. "What is the matter with you?"

"I don't understand myself," replied Bobby.

"Don't try to, 15/753. There isn't anything to understand. Just go about your job and try to be **useful**. The future will be built upon your loyalty. Above all, don't ask questions. The little word **why** has destroyed civilization after civilization."

Bobby buzzed agreement. His eyes lighted up as the head forager began to shore up his unsteady faith. The head forager noticed the brightening of the eyes.

"Yes, 15/753," the head forager continued with a voracious smile. "It is the highest wisdom not to ask questions. Once you ask questions you are bound sooner or later to make mistakes, and any one of them may be fatal."

"I am very grateful, sir," said Bobby, and he genuinely was relieved to be once more on the straight and narrow beeline that brings prosperity to the hive.

"Now off you go, 15/753," said the head forager bee in his most charming manner. "I don't suppose I'll ever have you up before me again."

"I hope not, sir," said Bobby.

On his next hour's outing he visited 323 flowers. This set up a hive record which was duly noted in the book, though Bobby was not thanked for it. He was happy enough to know that his belief in the race of bees and in the regulations had been proven beyond question. If the head forager believed in him it would have been madness for him to doubt himself.

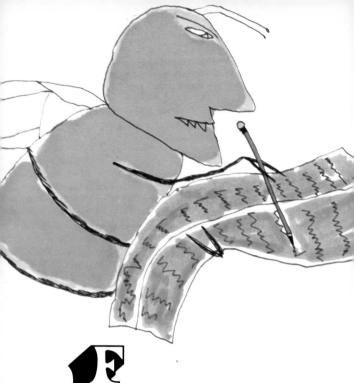

For a whole week he stayed away from Rosa. But as each day passed he longed to return and converse with her. Rosa was the only one who had given him a name and spoken to him without any thought of regulation-phrases and regulation-tones. At nights, in the midst of a huddled, snoring batch of bees he now felt lonely. He feared loneliness not

just because it hurt but because it meant—he hardly dared express it to himself—it meant that he was "out of place," didn't belong, was a stranger.

At last, though he knew it was wrong and would probably ruin him, he could resist the temptation no longer. For three quarters of an hour one afternoon he worked harder than he had ever worked. He ran up a total of 299 flowers. Then utterly exhausted

—for he had not been sleeping well—he asked Rosa if he could come in.

"Of course," she said melodiously. "I knew you'd come and visit me again."

For a while Bobby was too tired to speak. He was content to lie still, hidden in the perfumed folds of a bright red rose.

After five minutes of perfect peace, Bobby said, "Today I have learned what leisure is."

"You will never be the same again," Rosa murmured.

"I like your perfume." Bobby did not intend to flatter her. He thought that Rosa's scent was the sweetest he had ever smelled, indeed, the first he had really noticed.

"Ah," said Rosa wisely, "once you have recognized beauty you will find it hard to stay within your hive. Beauty takes no notice of rules; and in the

pursuit of beauty you will have to travel alone on an endless journey."

Bobby did not understand Rosa. He only knew that for the first time in his life he was happy. And unhappy.

"Rosa," he said without conviction, "my only aim in life is to be useful."

"No, Bobby," Rosa replied. "The only worthwhile aim in life is to bring joy."

"How do we bring joy?"

"By loving and caring. By giving someone a name that is his very own."

"Bees do not love or care for anyone," said Bobby sadly. "We never even go to the rescue of another hive when it's attacked. We cast out our sick and injured fellows so they perish in the cold night air."

"Then who are you being useful to?"

Bobby replied: "I do not know. That is a question we were warned we must never ask."

"Lie still," suggested Rosa, "and I will love and care for you."

At that moment, Bobby realized that his hour was nearly up. With a quick goodbye he renounced the invitation to joy and winged his way back to the hive.

"How many?" asked the doorkeeper.

"299. No, 300." Bobby had remembered Rosa. But he hadn't extracted any pollen from Rosa. It seemed a desecration to put Rosa on the list with the other nameless flowers. He corrected himself again. "Sorry," he said. "I was right the first time."

The doorkeeper was suspicious of Bobby's unusual hesitancy. He called the guards to arrest him. It wasn't like Bobby to make an error in his calculations.

A trial was arranged. The head forager presided. This time his long and ugly face was venomous.

"This is how you repay my kindness," he spat out, according to the regulations. "I have reason to suspect that you have been consorting with the enemy."

"Rosa is not an enemy. She is a beautiful flower."

"Ah," said the head forager. "So you admit you have been speaking to a flower."

"But she is not an enemy," insisted Bobby.

"The enemy is anyone who does not abide by our rules and regulations. The enemy is anyone who interferes with a bee's usefulness."

"Love," cried Bobby, "is higher than usefulness."

All the bees at the trial put their fingers in their ears until the word "love" had ceased to echo in the halls of the hive.

"You are impure," said the chief forager. "Soon you will be laying claims to happiness."

"I **am** laying claims to happiness. I am ashamed of the guilt I once felt at the mention of love and joy and pity. I sacrificed my future, your future, everybody's future, for **the** future that no one will ever enjoy.

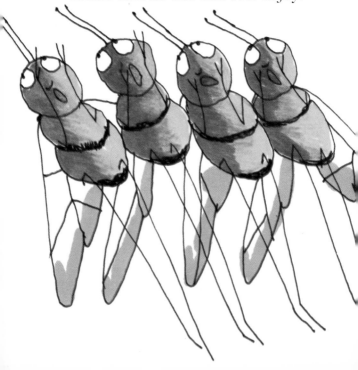

I let the guards destroy 19/201 who was my friend, and I did not lift a finger to help him."

"Silence," said the head forager.

"No, I won't," Bobby yelled back. "In my opinion the whole structure of the hive ought to be re-thought." Even Bobby was aware how ridiculous he was sounding. There wasn't a chance in a thousand million that **he** was right and the traditional pattern of the beehive wrong. But it was essential to his new loyalty to himself that he should affirm this evident absurdity. There was a certain dignity in demanding the right to be absurd.

For the sake of the other scandalized bees the head forager said, "Change one single element in our hive and there will be disorder and dissension. All of us would become unchaste, idle, avaricious. We would lose all sense of duty and be afraid to sacrifice ourselves for the sake of our fellow bees. We would end up like the race of human reasoners that slaughters its own kind."

"For a single spark of love, it would be worth it. If chaos is the price of love, let there be chaos."

There was certainly chaos in the judgment hall as Bobby yelled out his new-found faith. Love, it seemed, caused much more turmoil among the bees than swirling smoke.

The guards advanced upon him munching with their jaws. But each time they tried to lay hands on him Bobby cried aloud, "Love, love!" Immediately they all fell back holding their ears as if they were accursed. They could not attack him because all their energies were needed to protect themselves.

"Love, love!" shouted Bobby. He made his unimpaired exit from the

judgment hall and then from the hive itself shouting, "Love, love, love."

At the opening of the hive, the head forager, his hands over his ears, called after him:

"You cannot do without us, 15/753. **You know we are right.** Without us you will die."

Bobby despairingly cried out in return, "You are all dead already. If I die today at least I will die after having lived."

With that, Bobby went to join Rosa.

He felt lost and lonely. How was it, then, that he felt fully alive for the first time since he was hatched?

"Rosa," he said, "I'm cold and afraid," for night had fallen.

Rosa gladly permitted him to enter and warm himself in her sweet-smelling folds.

"Bobby," she said.

"Yes?" he asked, snuggling up in the heart of the rose.

"I am afraid, too."

"You must not be afraid of the bees' revenge. Remember, if they come, all you have to do is call out 'Love' and they will fly away."

"No, Bobby," Rosa whispered, "I'm not afraid of the bees. You see, it is almost the end of summer."

"And?"

"And I think my time is not very far away."

"Then," said Bobby bravely, "we will spend our last hours together loving and caring for each other."

So they did. When the sun came up in the early morning, it shone most brightly on the small stem of a blown red rose on which a bee lay dead.